The Dark

By

Leonid Andreev

The Dark
by Leonid Andreev

ISBN: 978-93-60461-94-2
Published by

DOUBLE 9 BOOKS

2/13-B, Ansari Road
Daryaganj, New Delhi – 110002
info@double9books.com
www.double9books.com
Tel. 011-40042856

ABOUT THE AUTHOR

Russian playwright, novelist, and short-story writer Leonid Nikolaievich Andreyev (21 August 1871 – 12 September 1919) is regarded as the founder of expressionism in Russian literature. He is recognized as one of the Silver Age literary period's most gifted and prolific writers. The components of the naturalist, symbolist, and realist literary schools are all combined in Andreyev's work. His play He Who Gets Slapped (1915) is considered his best play out of his 25 plays. Andreyev was raised in a middle-class household in Oryol, Russia, and first pursued his legal education in Saint Petersburg and Moscow. His mother claimed Finnish and Ukrainian ancestry in addition to coming from a wealthy yet ancient Polish noble family. He started working as a police-court reporter for a daily in Moscow, going about his menial work without drawing much notice to himself. He tried a few times to publish the poems he was writing at this period, but the majority of publishers turned him down. Maxim Gorky became aware of this tale and suggested Andreyev focus on his writing endeavors. After giving up his legal career, Andreyev quickly rose to fame in literature, and the two authors stayed close for a long time.

As a rule success had accompanied him in all his undertakings, but during the last three days complications had arisen which were unfavourable, not to say critical. His life, though a short one, had long been a game of terrible hazards; he was accustomed to these sudden turns of chance and could deal with them; the stake had before been life itself, his own and others', and this by itself had taught him alertness, swiftness of thought, and a cold hard outlook.

Chance this time had turned dangerously against him. A mere fluke, one of those unforeseeable accidents, had provided the police with a clue; for two whole days the detectives had been on his track, a known terrorist and nihilist, drawing the net ever closer round him. One after another the conspirators' hiding places had been cut off from him; there still remained to him a few streets and boulevards and restaurants where he might go undiscovered. But his terrible exhaustion, after two sleepless nights and days of ceaseless vigilance, had brought in its train a new danger: he might drop off to sleep anywhere, on a seat in the boulevards, even in a cab, and be ludicrously arrested as a common drunk.

It was now Tuesday. On Thursday—only one day to spare—he had to carry out a terrorist act of great importance. The preparations for the assassination had kept the little organization busy for some considerable time. The "honour" of throwing the last and decisive bomb had fallen to him. He must retain self-command at all costs.

But sleep....

It was thus, on that October evening, standing at the crossing of crowded streets, that he decided to take refuge in a brothel. He would have had recourse earlier to this refuge, though none too secure, had it not been for the good reason that all his twenty-six years he had been chaste, had never known women as mere women, had never been in a brothel. Now and then he had had to fight sternly against such desires, but gradually restraint had become habit, and had produced in him an attitude of calmness and complete indifference towards the sex. So now, at the thought of being forced into close contact with a woman who traded in such pleasures, and of perhaps seeing her naked, he had forebodings of any number of unpleasantnesses and awkward moments. True, he had only decided to go to a prostitute now, when his passion was quiescent, when a step had to be taken so important and serious that virginity and the struggle for it lost their value. But in any event it was unpleasant, as might be any other obnoxious incident which must be endured. Once, when assisting in an important act, in which he played the part of second bomb-thrower, he saw a horse which had been killed with its hind parts burst open and the entrails exposed; this incident, its filthy and disgusting character, and its needlessness, gave him a similar sensation—in its way even more unpleasant than the death of a comrade from an exploding bomb. And the more quietly and fearlessly, and even joyously, he anticipated Thursday, when he would probably have to die, the more was he oppressed with the prospect of a night with a woman who practised love as a profession, a thing utterly ridiculous, an incarnation of chaos, senseless, petty, and dirty.

But there was no alternative. He was tottering with fatigue.

It was still early when he arrived, about ten o'clock; but the great white hall with its gilded chairs and mirrors was ready for the reception of guests, and all the fires were lighted. The pianist was sitting beside the piano, a dapper young man in a black frock coat—for it was an expensive house. He was smoking, carefully flicking the ash of his cigarette so as not to soil the carpet, and glancing over the music. In the corner near the darkened dining room there sat all arow, on three chairs, three girls whispering to one another.

As he entered with the manageress, two of the girls rose, but the third remained sitting; the two who rose were very décolletée, the third wore a deep black frock. The two looked at him straight, with a look of invitation, half indifferent, half weary; but the third turned aside. Her profile was calm and simple, like that of any proper young maiden,—a thoughtful face. Apparently she had been telling a story to the others, and the others had been listening, and now she was continuing the train of thought, telling the rest in silence.

And just because she was silent and reflective and did not look at him, because she had the appearance of a proper woman, he chose her. Never before having been to a brothel he did not know that in every well equipped house of this sort there are one or two such women, dressed in black like nuns or young widows, with pale faces, unrouged, even stern, their task being to provide an illusion of propriety to those who seek it,— but when they go with a man to their room, drinking and becoming like the rest, or even worse,—brawling and breaking the china, dancing about, undressing and dancing into the hall naked, and even killing men who are too importunate. Such are the women with whom drunken students fall in love, whom they persuade to begin new, honourable lives.

But of all this he knew nothing. And when she rose reluctantly, and looked at him with displeased and averted eyes, glancing at him sharply out of her pale and colourless face, he thought once again, "How very proper she is!"—and felt some relief. But, keeping up the dissimulation, constant, unavoidable, which caused him to have two lives and made his life a stage, he balanced himself elegantly on his feet from his heels to his toes, snapped his fingers, and said to the girl with the careless air of a habitual debauchee:—

"Well, what about it, my dear? Shall we pay you a visit, now, eh? Where is your little nest?"

"Now—at once?" the girl asked, surprised, and raised her eyebrows. He smiled gaily, disclosing even rows of strong straight teeth, blushed deeply, and replied:

"Certainly. Why lose valuable time?"

"There will be some music soon. We can dance."

"Dance, my fair charmer? Silly twiddles,—catching oneself by the tail. As to the music, it can be heard from up there?"

She looked at him and smiled.

"Fairly well."

She was beginning to like him. He had prominent cheek bones and was clean shaven; his cheeks and the lower part of the mouth, under the clean-cut lips, were slightly blue, as when dark-bearded men shave. He had fine dark eyes, although in expression a little too unswerving; and they moved slowly and heavily, as though every movement were a great distance to be traversed. But despite his shaven face and easy manner, she reasoned, he did not resemble an actor, but rather an acclimatized foreigner.

"You are not a German?" she asked.

"Nnno. Not quite. I mean, I am an Englishman. Do you like Englishmen?"

"But what good Russian you speak! I should never have guessed!"

He recollected his British passport and the affected accent he had been using lately, and he blushed again at the thought of having forgotten to keep up the pretence as he ought to have done. Then with a slight frown, and assuming a business-like dryness of tone in which a certain amount of weariness was perceptible, he took the girl by the elbow and led her along swiftly.

"No, I am a Russian, Russian. Now, where are we to go? Show me! This way?"

The large mirror showed the full-length figures of the pair sharply and clearly—she in black, pale, and at that distance very pretty; he also in black, and just as pale.

Under the glare of the electric lights hanging from the ceiling his wide forehead and the hard mass of his prominent cheeks were peculiarly pale; and both in his face and the girl's, where the eyes should have been, there were mysterious, fascinating hollows. And so strange was the picture of such a black stern couple against the white walls, reflected in the broad gilded mirror, that he was startled, and stopped short by the thought: "Like a bride and bridegroom." And, as his imagination was dulled by want of sleep, and his thoughts brusque and inconsequent, the next moment, looking at the stern pair in mourning black, he thought: "As at a funeral." And both notions were equally unpleasant.

Apparently his feelings were shared by the girl. She silently, wonderingly glanced at herself and him, him and herself; she tried to wink—but the mirror would not respond to so slight a movement, and in the same dull and obstinate manner persisted in picturing this black shamefast couple. And perhaps this pleased the girl, or recalled something of herself, something sad, for she smiled gently, and lightly pressed his clenched hand.

"What a couple!" she said reflectively, and for some reason or other the dark bow of her eye-lashes, with the fine curve of their droop, became more noticeable.

This he did not observe, but resolutely dragged the girl along with him, she tapping her way on high French heels on the parquet flooring.

There was a corridor, as there always is, and narrow dark little rooms with open doors. At one of them inscribed above in irregular handwriting, "Liuba", they entered.

"And now, Liuba," he said, looking round and unconsciously rubbing his hands one over the other, as though carefully washing them in cold water, "don't we want wine and something else? Or some fruit?"

"Fruit is expensive here."

"That doesn't matter. Do you drink wine?"

He had forgotten himself and was addressing her as you; he noticed it, but did not correct himself, for there had been something in that touch of her hand which made him unwilling to use the familiar pronoun, or play the lover and act a part. This feeling, too, passed on to her; she stared at him fixedly, and answered deliberately, with some uncertainty in her voice, though none in the language she used.

"Thank you. I do drink. Wait a moment. I will return at once. I will tell them to bring only two pears and two apples. Will that be enough?"

It was now she who was using the pronoun of politeness, and through the tone of voice in which she spoke the word there could be heard the same irresolution, a slight hesitation and interrogation.

But he paid no attention to this. When he was alone, he went swiftly to work surveying the room from all sides. He tested the closing of the door—it closed splendidly, on the latch and on the key; went to the window, opened both casements—it was high up on the second floor and looked out on the courtyard. He frowned and shook his head. Then he experimented on the lights; there were two of them; when the one on the ceiling was switched off, the other by the bed lit up under a little red hood—just as in the best hotels.

But the bed!

He grinned and raised his shoulders, as though laughing silently, distorting his face as people must who are stealthy and for some reason secretive, even when they are alone.

But the bed!

He walked round it, handled the wadded counterpane, and then with a sudden longing to be gay and saucy in his joy at the sleep he was going to have, he twisted his head like a boy, stuck out his lips, made round eyes—all to express his highest degree of amazement. But at once he became serious again, sat down, and wearily waited for Liuba.

He wanted to think of Thursday, that he was now in a brothel—that he was already there—but the thought rebelled and stubbornly resisted him. Outraged sleep was taking its revenge. There on the street, sleep had been so gentle; now it no longer caressed his face, as with a soft downy hand, but made his own hands and feet writhe, and racked his body as though it would rend him asunder.

Suddenly he began yawning, even to the point of tears. He took out his Browning and three full clips of cartridges, and savagely blew down the barrel, as into a key. It was all in order ... and he longed insufferably for sleep.

When the wine and fruit were brought in, and Liuba came in after them, he shut the door, only on the latch, and said:

"Well ... all right ... please help yourself, Liuba. Please do."

"And you ...?" The girl, surprised, looked at him askance.

"I will ... later on. For two nights, you see, I have been having a gay time of it and have had no sleep, and now...." He yawned frightfully, straining his jaws.

"Well...?"

"I will ... later. Just an hour. I will ... soon. And you, please drink and don't spare. And eat the fruit. Why did you get so little?"

"But may I go into the hall? There will be some music."

This was inconvenient. They might begin talking about him, the strange guest who had gone to sleep, and might start guessing ... and that might be awkward. So, lightly restraining a yawn which was already riving his jaws, he said sedately and earnestly:

"No, Liuba. I shall ask you to stay here. You see, I don't much like sleeping alone in a room. It's a mere whim, but you will excuse me...."

"Certainly. You have paid your money and...."

"Yes, yes," and he blushed for the third time, "quite true, but that isn't what I mean.... And, if you like ... you can lie down too. I will leave room for you. Only please lie next the wall. You don't mind?"

"No, I don't want to sleep. I will just sit here."

"Will you read?"

"There are no books here."

" Would you like today's paper? I have it here. There is something interesting in it."

"No, thank you."

"As you like. You know best. But ... with your permission...."

He shut and locked the door and put the key in his pocket, without noticing the strange look with which the girl followed his movements. This courteous and decent conversation, such a curious conversation in this home of misery where the very air was thick with the vapours of drunken brawls, seemed to him perfectly natural and quite convincing. With the same polite air, as though he were in the company of young ladies, he touched the edge of his frock-coat and asked:

"Do you mind if I take off my coat?"

The girl scowled slightly.

"Certainly. Of course...."

"And my waistcoat? It's so tight."

The girl did not answer, but merely shrugged her shoulders.

"Here is my pocket-book ... and money. Will you be so good as to take care of them for me?"

"You had better leave them at the office. We always deposit such things there."

"Why?" He looked at the girl, and turned aside in confusion. "Oh, of course ... but that's silly!"

"But do you know how much you have on you? Some people don't know, and then afterwards...."

"I understand. Quite. You desire...."

He lay down, politely leaving room for her by the wall. And enchanting sleep, spaciously smiling, came and nestled with its downy cheek against his, gently fondled him, stroking his knees, and mercifully settling to rest with its soft, velvety head on his shoulder. He smiled.

"What makes you smile?" The girl smiled involuntarily.

"Because I am comfortable.... How soft your pillows are! Now we can talk awhile. Why don't you drink something?"

"I think I shall take off my things ... if you don't mind? I shall have to sit still so long."

Her voice had a touch of mockery. But at the sight of his unsuspecting glance, and hearing his simple.... "Certainly, please do" ... she explained quite simply and seriously: "My corset is so tight. I shall take it off, too ... if I may."

"Certainly, you may."

He turned away, blushing. But, either because insomnia had so addled his thoughts, or because all his life he had been so innocent, his "you may" sounded quite natural to him ... in a house where all things were allowed and nobody ever thought of asking anybody's leave about anything.

He heard a rustling of silk and the unbuttoning of a dress,—then a question:

"You are not an author?"

"What ... an author? No, I am not an author. Er ... do you like authors?"

"No, I do not."

"Why? They are men...." He yawned—a long satisfying yawn.

"And what is your name?"

Silence ... and then:

"My name is ... N—no! Peter."

"And what are you? What do you do?"

The girl questioned him gently, but watchfully, and in a firm tone. The impression conveyed by her voice might have been that she was moving towards the bed. But he by now had ceased to hear her; he was already sleeping. For one moment an expiring thought had flickered in a single picture, in which time and space melted into a motley of shadows, gloom and light, motion and repose, a single picture of crowds and endless streets and a ceaseless turning of wheels depicted the whole of those two days and nights of frenzied chase. And in an instant all of this was stilled, dimmed, and had passed away, and then in the soft half-light, in the deep shadow, he had an image of one of the picture galleries where, the day before, for two hours, he had eluded his pursuers. He seemed to be sitting on a red velvet divan, which was extraordinarily soft, and staring fixedly at a huge black picture; and such a restfulness proceeded from that old black cracked canvas, his eyes were so much rested, his thoughts reposing so gently, that for some moments, even in his sleep, he began fighting sleep, confusedly afraid of it, as though of an unknown disquietude.

But the music in the hall played on, the frequent little notes with bare heads hairless jostled up and down, and the thought came: "Now I can sleep." And all at once he fell into a deep slumber. Triumphantly, eagerly, gentle glossy sleep soothed and embraced him and in profound silence masking their breathing they went their way into a pellucid melting sea.

Thus he slept on—one hour and then another—on his back in the polite posture he had assumed awake, his right hand in his pocket holding the key and his revolver; the girl, neck and arms bare sitting opposite, smoking, sipping cognac, gazing on him. Now and then, to get a better view, she craned her rather thin, flexible neck, and, when she moved, her lips curled with two deep creases of constraint. She had not thought to turn out the hanging lamp, and under the strong light he was neither young nor old nor strange nor intimate, but some unknown being—the cheeks unknown, the nose ending in a bird's beak of shape unknown, the breathing, so even and powerful and strong, unknown. His thick hair was cut short in military fashion, and she noticed on the left temple, near the eye, a little whitened scar from some former wound. There was no cross strung round his neck.

The music in the hall died down or started afresh—piano and violin and songs and the pit-a-pat of dancing feet; but she sat on, smoking cigarettes and observing the sleeper. She stretched her neck inquisitively to look at his left hand which was lying on his breast —a very broad palm and strong restful fingers; it seemed to weigh heavily on him, to hurt, so with a careful movement she lifted it and let it down gently at the side of the big body on the bed. Then rose swiftly and noisily, and, as though she wanted to smash the switch, roughly turned out the upper lamp, lighting the lower one under the red hood.

But even then he did not stir. His face in the pink light remained as unknown, as terrifying as before, in its immobility and repose.

She turned aside, clasped her knees with her arms, now softly reddening, threw her head back and stared motionless at the ceiling from the dusky hollows of her unblinking eyes. And in her teeth, tightly pressed, there hung a cigarette, half smoked, cold, dead.

Something had happened, something unexpected and terrible, something considerable and of consequence, whilst he was sleeping—this much he understood at a flash, even before he was properly awake, at the first sound of a harsh, unknown voice. He took it in with that sharpened sense of danger which to him and his comrades had developed almost into a new special sense. He was up quickly and sat with his hand pressing his revolver hard, his eyes searchingly and sharply exploring the mist of the room. And when he saw her, in the same attitude, with her shoulders of that transparent rosy hue, and her bared breast, and those eyes so enigmatically dark and unswerving, he thought to himself: "She has betrayed me!" Then he looked again more steadily, sighed deeply, and corrected himself: "She hasn't yet, but she will."

How miserable it all was!

He drew a deep breath and asked curtly: "Well, what is it?"

She said nothing. She smiled triumphantly and spitefully, looked at him and was silent,—as though she already accounted him her own, and without haste or hurry wanted to gloat over her power.

"What did you say just now?" he repeated, with a frown.

"What I said? I said, get up!—that's what I said. Get up! You 've been asleep. It's time to play the game. This isn't a doss-house, my dear!"

"Tum on the light," he commanded.

"I will not."

He turned it on himself, and under the white light he saw her eyes infinitely wicked and black and painted, and her mouth compressed with hatred and disdain. And he saw the naked arms, and all of her, alien, decisive, ready to do something irrevocable. He saw the prostitute—a creature repellant to him.

"What's the matter with you? Are you drunk?" he asked, seriously disquieted, and put out a hand to take his high starched collar. But, anticipating his movement, she snatched at the collar, and without looking hurled it somewhere, anywhere, into the room, behind the chest of drawers, into a corner.

"I won't give it to you!"

"What are you after now?" he asked calmly enough, but gripping her arm with a hard firm pressure all round like an iron ring, so that the fingers of her thin hand drooped powerlessly.

"Let go! You're hurting me!" she cried, and he held her more gently, but did not release his hold.

"You—look for it!"

"What is it, my dear? Are you going to shoot me? Isn't that a revolver you have in your pocket? Well, shoot, shoot! I'll see how you shoot me! Or would you like to tell me why you take a woman and then go to sleep by yourself and tell her to drink—'Drink, and I'll go to sleep!' With his hair cut and clean shaven, so that he thinks nobody will know him! Do you want to go to the police, my dear? To the police, eh?"

She laughed, loud and merrily—and in a way that really frightened him, there was such a savage, despairing joy on her face, as though she had gone mad. And then the idea that all was going to be lost in such a ludicrous fashion, that he would have to commit this silly, cruel, and senseless murder, and yet himself probably perish in vain, struck him with even greater horror. Deadly pale, but externally calm and with the same resolute air, he looked at her, followed her every movement and word, collecting his thoughts.

"Well? Silent now? Lost your tongue?"

He could seize this snaky neck and crush it and she would never be able to utter a shriek. He could do it without compunction; actually, while he held her so firmly, she had been twisting herself about like a snake.

"So you know, Liuba, what I am?"

"I do. You"—she enunciated the words syllable by syllable, harshly and with an air of triumph—"you are a revolutionary! That's what you are!"

"How do you know?"

She smiled mockingly.

"We aren't quite in the backwoods here."

"Well, suppose we admit that I...."

"Pooh, suppose we admit! Let go of my arm! You're all alike, you men, always ready to use your strength against a woman. Let go!"

He released her arm and sat down, looking at her with a heavy and obstinate wonder. Something was moving about his cheekbones, a little ball of muscle, with a disturbed motion; but his expression was tranquil, serious, somewhat melancholy. And this made him again seem strange and unknown to her—and also very handsome.

"Well, will you know me again?" she exclaimed, and surprised herself by adding a coarse reproof. He raised his brows in surprise and spoke to her calmly, but without averting his eyes, dully, remotely, as from a great distance.

"Listen, Liuba, certainly you can betray me, not only you, but anyone in this house, or in the street. One shout—Halt! arrest him!—and men will come in their tens and hundreds and try to get me—or kill me. And for what reason? Merely because I have done no harm, merely because I have devoted all my life to these very people. Do you understand what it means, to sacrifice one's life?"

"No, I do not," the girl retorted harshly, but listening attentively.

"Some do it out of stupidity, some for spite. Because, Liuba, a common man cannot endure a fine man, and the wicked do not love the good...."

"What should they love them for?"

"Don't think, Liuba, that I am simply praising myself. But just look what my life has been, what it is! From the age of fourteen I have been rubbing along in prisons, expelled from school, expelled from home. My parents drove me out. Once I was nearly shot dead, saved only by a miracle. Try to picture it—all one's life passed in this way, all for the sake of others, and for oneself, nothing—yes, nothing!"

"And what induced you to be so ... fine?" she asked jeeringly. But he replied seriously:

"I don't know. I must have been born so."

"And I was born such a common sort of thing! And yet I came into the world the same way you did, didn't I?"

But he was not listening. All his mind was held by the vision of his own past, so unexpectedly, so simply heroic, called up by his own words.

"Yes ... think of it ... I'm 26 years old and there are already grey hairs on my head, and yet until today ..." he hesitated a moment and went on firmly, proudly. "Up to now I have never known a woman.... Never ... do you understand? You are the first I even see ... like that. And to tell the truth, I am just a little ashamed to be looking at your bare arms."

The music rose again wildly, and the floor vibrated with the rhythm of dancing feet, broken by a drunken man's wild whoop, as though he were heading off a herd of stampeding horses. But in the room it was still, and the tobacco smoke rose serenely and melted into a ruddy mist.

"That is what my life has been, Liuba!"

He looked down, thoughtfully and sternly, overcome by the thought of a life so pure, so painfully beautiful. And she made no reply.

Then she got up and threw a wrap around her bare shoulders. But at the sight of his look of astonishment, almost gratitude, she smiled and brusquely threw the wrap off, and so arranged her chemise that one breast, rosy and soft, was left bared. He turned away and slightly shrugged his shoulders.

"Take a drink!" she said.

"No, I never drink anything."

"What, never drink! But you see, I do!"

"If you've got some cigarettes, I'll have one."

"They're very common ones."

"I don't care."

And when he took the cigarette he noticed with pleasure that Liuba had put her chemise straight, and the hope that everything might yet go smoothly rose again. He was a poor smoker; he did not inhale, and womanlike held the cigarette between two straight fingers.

"You don't even know how to smoke!" the girl exclaimed angrily, and roughly tried to snatch the cigarette from him. "Throw it away!"

"Now, there you are,—angry with me again!"

"Yes, I am!"

"But why, Liuba? Just think! For two nights I haven't had any sleep, running about the town from pillar to post. And now, you're going to give me up and they'll have me in jail! That's a fine finish, isn't it? But, Liuba, I'll never give in alive...."

He stopped short.

"Will you shoot?"

"Yes, I shall shoot."

The music had ceased for a time, but the wild drunken man was still halloing although apparently someone, as a joke or in earnest, had a hand on his mouth, the sounds coming through the compressed fingers even more desperately and savagely. The room reeked no longer with cheap fragrant soap, but with a thick, moist and repulsive odour; on one wall, uncovered, there hung messily and flat some petticoats and blouses. It was all so repugnant, so strange, to think that this also was life,—that people were living such a life day in, day out,—that he felt dazed and shrugged his shoulders and again looked round slowly.

"What a place this is!" he said, bemused and resting his eyes on Liuba.

"What of it?" she asked curtly.

He looked at her as she stood there, and suddenly understood that she was to be pitied; and as soon as he had grasped this he did pity her—ardently.

"You are poor, Liuba?"

"Well?"

"Give me your hand."

And, as though to assert in some way his relation to the girl as a human being, he took her hand and respectfully raised it to his lips.

"You mean that ... for me?"

"Yes, Liuba, for you."

Then quite quietly, as though thanking him, she said:

"Off you go! Get out of here, you block-head!"

He did not understand at once.

"What?"

"Off with you. Get out of here! Get out!"

Silently, with a steady step, she crossed the room, picked up the white collar in the corner, and threw it to him with an expression of disgust, as though it had been the dirtiest, filthiest rag. And he, likewise silent, but with an expression of high resolve, without sparing even one glance at the girl, began quietly and slowly buttoning on the collar; but all in a moment, with a savage whine, Liuba struck him on his shaven cheek, with all her strength. The collar fell on the floor; he was shaken from his balance, but steadied himself. Pale, almost blue, but still silent, with the same look of lofty composure and proud incomprehension, he faced her with a stolid, unswerving stare. She was drawing rapid breaths, and staring at him in terror.

"Well?" she gasped.

He looked at her, still silent.

Then, maddened beyond endurance by his haughty unresponsiveness, terror-stricken by the stone wall against which she seemed to have flung herself, the girl lost all control of herself and seizing him by the shoulders forcibly thrust him down upon the bed. She bent over him, her face near his, and eye to eye.

"Well? Why don't you answer? What are you trying to do with me? You scoundrel—that's what you are! Kiss my hand, will you? Come here to boast of yourself, will you? To show off your beauty! What are you trying to do with me? Do you think I'm so happy?"

She shook him by the shoulders, and her thin fingers, unconsciously curling and uncurling like a cat's claws, scratched his body through his shirt.

"And he's never known a woman, hasn't he? You brute, you dare come here and brag about this to me—to me for whom any man is simply.... Where's your decency? What do you think you're doing with me? "I'll never give in alive." That's the tune is it? But I—of course, I'm already dead. You understand, you rascal? I'm dead! But I spit in your face ... ph!... in the face of the living! There! Get out, you brute! Get out of here!"

With anger he could no longer command, he threw her off him and she fell backwards against the wall. Apparently his mind was still confused, for his next movement, equally rapid and decisive, was to seize his revolver and look at its grinning, toothless mouth. But the girl never so much as saw his bespattered face, damp and disfigured with demoniac rage, nor the black revolver. She covered her eyes with her hands, as though to crush them into the farthest recesses of her brain, stepped forward swiftly and steadily, and flung herself on the bed, face down, in a fit of silent sobbing.

Everything had turned out different from what he had anticipated. Out of vapidity and nonsense there had crept forth a chaos—savage, drunken, and hysterical, with a crumpled, distorted face.

He shrugged his shoulders, put away the useless revolver, and began pacing the room, up and down. The girl was crying.

To and fro again. The girl was crying. He stopped beside her, his hands in his pockets, to look at her.

There, under his eyes, face down, lay a woman sobbing frantically in an agony of unbearable sorrow, sobbing as one who looks suddenly back on a wasted life or a better life irretrievably lost. Her naked, finely tapering shoulder blades were heaving as though to heap fuel on the raging furnace within, and sinking as though to compress the tense anguish in her bosom.

The music had started afresh; a mazurka now. And the jingle of spurs could be heard. Some officers must have come.

Such tears he had never seen! He was disconcerted. He took his hands out of his pockets, and said gently:

"Liuba!"

Still she sobbed.

"Liuba! What is the matter, Liuba?"

She answered, but so faintly that he could not hear. He sat by her on the bed, bent his shorn head, and laid a hand on her shoulders; and his hand responded with a quiver to the trembling of those pitiable shoulders.

"I can't hear what you say, Liuba?"

Then something distant, dull, soaked in tears:

"Wait—before you go ... over there ... some officers have arrived. They might see you ... My God—to think...!"

She sat up quickly on the bed, clasping her hands, eyes wide open staring into space in sudden fear. The terror lasted a moment, and then she again lay down and wept. Outside the spurs were jingling rhythmically, and the pianist with revived energy was conscientiously beating out a vigorous mazurka.

"Take a drink of water, Liuba, do I You really must ... please ..." he whispered as he bent over her. Her ear was covered with her hair, and fearing that she could not hear, he carefully brushed aside those dark curling locks, and discovered a hot little red shell of an ear.

"Please drink! I beg you!"

"No, I don't want a drink. There's no need.... It's all over."

She had quieted down by now. The sobbing stopped; one more long throe, and the shuddering shoulders were pathetically still; he was gently stroking her neck down to the lace of the chemise.

"Are you better, Liuba?"

She said nothing, but heaved a long sigh and turned round, quickly glancing at him. Then she relaxed and sat up, looked up at him again, and rubbed his face and eyes with the plaits of her hair. She breathed another long sigh and quite gently and simply laid her head on his shoulder, and he as simply put an arm round her and drew her silently closer to him. His fingers touched her naked shoulder, but this no longer disturbed him. And thus they sat a long while without speaking, but with now and then a sigh, staring straight ahead of them into space with unseeing eyes.

Suddenly there was a sound of voices and steps in the corridor, a jingling of spurs, quite gentle and elegant, like that of young officers. The sound came nearer and halted at the door. He rose promptly. Someone was knocking at the door, first tapping with knuckles and then banging with their fists, and a woman's voice called out:

"Liubka, open the door!"

He looked at her and waited.

"Give me a handkerchief," she said, without looking at him, and put her hand out. She rubbed her face hard, blew her nose noisily, threw the handkerchief on his knees, and went to the door. He watched and waited. On her way to the door she turned out the light, and it was all at once so dark that he could hear his own rather laboured breathing. And for some reason he sat down again on the creaking bed.

"Well? What is it? What do you want?" she asked through the door, without opening it, her voice calm, but still betraying some uneasiness.

Feminine voices were heard in argument and, cutting through them as scissors cut through a tangle of silk, a male voice, young, persuasive, seeming to proceed from behind strong white teeth and a soft moustache. Spurs jingled as though the speaker were responding with a bow. And—strange!—Liuba smiled.

"No. No! I don't want to come—Very well, do as you like. No, not for all your 'lovely Liubas'. I won't come." Another knock at the door, laughter, a sound of scolding, more jingling of spurs, and it all moved away from the door, and died out somewhere down the corridor. In the dark, fumbling for his knee with her hand, Liuba sat down by him, but did not lay her head on his shoulder. She explained briefly:

"The officers are starting a dance. They are summoning everybody. They are going to have a cotillion."

"Liuba," he said, pleadingly, "please turn on the light. Don't be angry."

She got up without a word and switched it on. And now she no longer sat with him but, as before, on the chair facing the bed. Her face was surly, uninviting, but courteous—like that of a hostess who cannot help sitting through an uninvited and overlong visit.

"You are not angry with me, Liuba?"

"No. Why should I be?"

"I wondered just now when you laughed so merrily."

She laughed without looking up.

"When I feel merry, I laugh. But you can't leave just now. You'll have to wait until the officers get away. It won't be long."

"Very well. I will wait, thank you, Liuba."

She laughed again.

"How courteous you are!"

"Don't you like it?"

"Not too well. What are you by birth?"

"My father is a doctor in the military service. My grandfather was a peasant. We are old-ritualists."

Liuba, surprised, looked up at him.

"Really? But you don't wear a cross round your neck."

"A cross!" he laughed. "We wear our cross on our backs."

The girl frowned slightly.

"You want to go to sleep? You'd better lie down than waste time in this way."

"No, I won't lie down. I don't want to sleep any more."

"As you wish."

There was a long and awkward silence. Liuba gazed downwards and fixed her attention on turning a ring on her finger. He looked round the room; each time be conspicuously avoided meeting the girl's glance, and rested his eyes on the unfinished glass of cognac. Then, all at once, it became overwhelmingly clear to him, even palpably evident, that all this was no longer what it seemed—that little yellow glass with the cognac, the girl so absorbed in twiddling her ring—and he himself, too, he was no longer himself, but someone else, someone alien and quite apart.... Just then the music stopped and there followed a quiet jingle of spurs.... He seemed to himself to have lived at some time, not in this house, but in a place very much like it; and that he had been an active and even important person to whom something was now happening. That strange feeling was so powerful that he shuddered and shook his head; and the feeling soon left him, but not altogether; there remained some faint inexpungible trace of the turbulent memories of that which had never been. And quite often, in the course of this unusual night, he caught himself at a point whence he was looking down on some object or person, trying anxiously to recall them out of the deep darkness of the past, even out of what had never existed.

Had he not known it for a thing impossible, he would have said that he had already been here on some occasion, so familiar and habitual had it all become. And this was unpleasant; it had already imperceptibly estranged him from himself and his comrades, and mysteriously made him a part of this institution, part of its wild and loathesome life.

Silence became oppressive.

"Why aren't you drinking?" he asked.

She shivered.

"What?"

"You haven't finished your glass, Liuba. Why don't you?"

"I don't want to by myself."

"I'm sorry, but I don't drink."

"And I don't drink by myself."

"I would rather eat a pear."

"Pray do so. They are here for that purposes."

"Wouldn't you like a pear?"

The girl did not answer, but turned aside and caught his glance resting on her naked and translucently rosy shoulders, and flung a grey knitted shawl over them.

"It's rather cold," she said abruptly.

"Yes, a little cold," he agreed, although it was very warm in that little room.

And again there was a long and tense silence. From the hall could be heard the catchy rhythm of a noisy *ritornello*.

"They are dancing," he said.

"They are dancing," she replied.

"What was it made you so angry with me, that you struck me, Liuba?"

The girl hesitated and then answered sharply.

"There was nothing else for it so I struck you. I didn't kill you, so why make a fuss about it?"

Her smile was ugly.

There was nothing else for it? She was looking straight at him with her dark rounded eyes, with a pallid and determined smile. Nothing else for it? He noticed a little dimple in her chin. It was hard to believe that this same head, this evil pallid head, had been lying on his shoulder a minute or two ago, that he had been caressing her!

"So that's the reason," he said gloomily. He paced to and fro in the room once or twice, but not toward the girl; and when he sat down again in the same place his face wore a strangely sullen and rather haughty expression. He said nothing, but, raising his eyebrows, stared at the ceiling where there played a spot of light with red edges. Something was crawling across it, something small and black, probably a belated autumn fly, revived by the heat. It had been brought to life in the night, and certainly understood nothing and would soon die. He sighed.

But now she laughed aloud.

"What is there to make you merry?" He looked up coldly and turned aside.

"I suppose—you are very much like the author. You don't mind? He too at first pities me, and then gets angry, because I do not adore him as though he were an icon. He's so touchy. If he were God, he'd never forgive even one candle," she smiled.

"But how do you know any authors? You don't read anything."

"There is one ..." she said curtly.

He pondered, fixing on the girl his unswerving gaze, too calm in its scrutiny. Living in a turmoil himself, he began vaguely to recognize in the girl a rebellious spirit; and this agitated him and made him try to puzzle out why it was that her wrath had fallen on him. The fact that she had dealings with authors, and probably talked with them, that she could sometimes assume such an air of quiet dignity and yet could speak with such malice— all this gave her interest and endowed her blow with the character of something more earnest and serious than the mere hysterical outburst of a half-drunk, half-naked prostitute. At first he had been only indignant, not offended; but now, in this interval of reflection, he was gradually becoming affronted, and this not only intellectually.

"Why did you hit me, Liuba? When you strike anyone in the face, you should tell them why."

He repeated his question sullenly and persistently. Obstinacy and stony hardness were expressed in his prominent cheekbones and the heavy brow that overshadowed his eyes.

"I don't know," she replied with the same obduracy, but avoiding his gaze.

She did not wish to answer him. He shrugged his shoulders, and again went on, pertinaciously staring at the girl and weaving his fancies. His thought, usually sluggish, once aroused worked forcibly and could not be deterred—worked almost mechanically, turning into something like a hydraulic press which slowly sinking powders up stones and bends iron beams and crushes anyone that falls beneath it—slowly, indifferently, irresistibly. Turning neither to the left nor to the right, unmoved by sophisms, evasions, allusions, his thought would push forward clumsily and heavily until it ground itself down or reached the logical extreme beyond which lay the void and mystery. He did not dissociate his thought from himself; he thought integrally, with the whole of his body; and each logical deduction forthwith became real to him—as happens only with very healthy or direct persons who have not yet turned thought into a pastime. And now, alarmed, driven out of his course, like a heavy locomotive that has slipped its rails on a pitch dark night and by some miracle continues leaping over hillocks and knolls, he was seeking a road and could not anyhow find it. The girl was still silent and evidently did not wish to talk.

"Liuba, let us have a quiet talk. We must try to...."

"I don't want to have a quiet talk."

Then again:

"Listen, Liuba. You hit me, and I cannot let matters rest at that."

The girl smiled.

"No? What will you do with me? Go to the police-court?"

"No, but I shall keep coming to you until you explain."

"You will be welcome. Madame gets her profit."

"I shall come tomorrow. I shall come...."

And then, suddenly, almost simultaneously with the thought that neither tomorrow nor the day after would he be able to come, there flashed upon him the surmise, almost certainty, why the girl had struck him. His face cleared.

"Oh, that's it then! That's why you struck me—because I pitied you? I offended you with my compassion? Yes, it is very stupid ... but really, I didn't mean to—though of course it hurts. After all, you are human, just as I am...."

"Just as you are?" she smiled.

"Well, let that pass. Give me your hand. Let's be friends."

She turned pale.

"You want me to smack your face again?"

"Give me your hand—as friends—as friends," he repeated sincerely, but for some reason in a low voice.

But Liuba got up, and moving a little distance away said:

"Do you know ... either you are a fool or you have been very little beaten!"

She looked at him and laughed aloud.

"My God, yes! My author! A most perfect author! How could one help hitting you, my dear?"

She apparently chose the word author purposely, and with some special and definite meaning. And then, with supreme disdain, taking no more account of him than of a chattel or hopeless imbecile or drunkard, she walked freely up and down, and jeered:

"Or was it that I hit you too hard? What are you whining about?"

He made no reply.

"My author says that I'm a hard fighter. Perhaps he has a finer face. However hard one smacks your cheeks you seem to feel nothing! Oh, I've knocked lots of people's mouths about, but I've never been so sorry for anyone as for my author. 'Hit away', he says, 'I deserve it.' A drunken slobberer! It's disgusting hitting him. He's a brute. But I hurt my hand on your face. Here—kiss it where it smarts!"

She thrust her hand to his lips and withdrew it swiftly. Her excitement was increasing. For some minutes it seemed as though she were choking in a fever; she rubbed her breast, breathing deeply through her open mouth, and unconsciously gripped the window curtains. And twice she stopped as she went to and fro to pour out a glass of cognac. The second time he remarked in a surly tone.

"You said you didn't drink alone."

"I have no consistency, my dear," she replied, quite simply. "I'm drugged, and unless I drink at intervals I stifle ... This revives me."

Then all at once, as if she had only just noticed him, she raised her eyes in surprise, and laughed.

"Ah! There you are—still there! Not gone yet! Sit down, sit down!" With a savage light in her eyes, she threw off the knitted wrap, again baring her rosy shoulders and thin soft arms. "Why am I all wrapped up like this? It's hot here and I ... I must have been saving him! How kind!... Look here, you might at least take your trousers off. It's only good manners here to do without your trousers. If your drawers are dirty I'll give you mine. Oh, never mind the slit. Here, put them on. Now, my dear boy, you must, you'll have to...."

She laughed until she choked, begging and putting out her hands. Then she knelt down, clasping his hands, and implored him: —

"Now, my darling, do! And I'll kiss your hand!"

He moved away, and, with an air of sullen grief, said:

"What are you trying to do with me, Liuba? What have I done to you? My relations with you are quite proper. I'm being perfectly decent to you. What are you doing? What is it? Have I offended you? If I have, forgive me. You know, I am ... I don't know about these things."

With a contemptuous shrug of her naked shoulders, Liuba rose from her knees and sat down, breathing heavily.

"You mean you won't put them on."

"I'm sorry, but I should look...."

He began saying something, hesitated and continued irresolutely, drawling his words.

"Listen, Liuba.... It's quite true! ... It's all such nonsense! But, if you wish it, then we can put out the light? Yes, put out the light, please, Liuba."

"What?" The girl's eyes opened wide in bewilderment.

"I mean," he continued hurriedly, "that you are a woman and I am ... certainly I was in the wrong.... Don't think it was compassion, Liuba. No, really it wasn't. Really not, Liuba. I ... but turn out the light, Liuba."

With an agitated smile he put out his hands to her in the clumsy caressing way of a man who has never had to do with women. And this is what he saw: she clenched her fists with a slow effort and raised them to her chin and became, as it were, one immense gasp contained in her swelling bosom, her eyes huge and staring with horror and anguish and inexpressible contempt.

"What is the matter, Liuba?" he asked, shattered. And with a cold horror, without unclasping her fingers, almost inaudibly she exclaimed:

"Oh, you brute! My God, what a brute you are!"

Crimson with the shame of the reproof, and outraged in that he had himself committed outrage, he stamped furiously on the floor and hurled abuse in rough curt words at those wide staring eyes with their unfathomable terror and pain.

"You prostitute, you! You refuse! Silence! Silence!"

But she still quietly shook her head and repeated:

"My God! My God! What a brute you are."

"Silence, you slut! You're drunk. You've gone mad! Do you think I need your filthy body? Do you think it's for such as you that I've kept myself? Sluts like you ought to be flogged!" And he lifted his hand as though to box her ears, but did not touch her.

"My God! My God!"

"And they even pity you! You ought to be extirpated, all this abomination and vice! Those who go with you, too—all that rabble! And you dare to think me anything of that sort!"

He roughly took her by the hand and flung her on the chair.

"Oh, you fine man! Fine? Fine, are you?" She laughed in a transport of delight.

"Fine? Yes. All my life! Honourable! Pure! But you? What are you, you harlot, you miserable beast?"

"A fine man!" The delight of it was intoxicating her.

"Yes, fine. After tomorrow I shall be going to my death, for mankind, for you ... and you? You'll be sleeping with my executioners. Call your officers in here! I'll fling you at their feet and tell them, 'Take your carrion!' Call them in!"

Liuba slowly rose to her feet, and when, in a tempest of emotion, with proud distended nostrils, he looked at her, he was met by a look as proud and even more disdainful. Even pity shone in the arrogant eyes of the prostitute; she had mounted miraculously a step of the invisible throne and thence, with a cold and stern attention, gazed down on something at her feet—something petty, clamorous, pitiable. She no longer smiled; there was no trace of excitement; her eyes involuntarily seemed to look for the little step on which she was standing, so conscious was she of the new height from which she looked down on all things beneath her.

"What are you?" he repeated, without moving away, as vehement as ever, but already subdued by that calm, haughty gaze.

Then, with an ominous air of conviction, behind which lay a vista of millions of crushed lives and oceans of bitter tears and the unchecked fiery course of rebellion's cry for justice, she asked sternly:

"What right have you to be fine when I am so common?"

"What?" he did not understand at once, but instantly felt a dread of the gulf that yawned in all its blackness at his very feet.

"I have been waiting for you for a long time."

"You—waiting for me?"

"Yes, I have been waiting for a fine man. For five years I have been waiting—perhaps longer. All those who came admitted they were brutes—and brutes they were. My author first said he was fine, but then admitted he was a brute, too. I don't want that sort."

"What, then—what do you want?"

"I want you, my darling,—you. Yes, just such as you." She scrutinized him carefully and quietly from head to foot and affirmatively nodded her head. "Yes—thank you for coming."

Then he who feared nothing, trembled.

"What do you want with me?" he asked, stepping back.

"It had to be a fine man, my dear, a really fine man. Those other drivellers—its no good striking them—you only dirty your hands. But now that I have struck you—why, I can kiss my own hand! Little hand, you have hit a fine man!" She smiled, and did in fact three times stroke and kiss her right hand.

He looked at her wildly, and his usually deliberate thoughts coursed with the speed of desperation. There was approaching, like a black cloud, a Thing, terrible and irreparable as death.

"What—what did you say?"

"I said it's shameful to be fine. Didn't you know that?"

"I never—" he muttered, and sat down, deeply confused and no longer fully conscious of her.

"Then learn it now."

She spoke calmly, and only the swelling of her half-bared bosom betrayed how profound the emotion was that lay suppressed behind that myriad cry.

"Do you realise it now?"

"What?" He was recovering himself.

"Do you realise it, I say?"

"Have patience!"

"I am patient, my dear. I have waited five years. Why shouldn't I be patient for another five minutes?"

She sat back comfortably on the chair, as though in anticipation of a rare pleasure, and crossed her naked arms and closed her eyes.

"You say it's shameful to be fine?"

"Yes, my pet, shameful."

"But—what you say is...." He stopped short in terror.

" ... is so! Are you afraid? Never mind, never mind—it's only at first that it's frightening."

"But afterwards?"

"You are going to stay with me and learn what comes afterwards."

He did not understand.

"How can I stay?"

The girl, in her turn, was startled.

"Can you go anywhere now, after this? Look, dear, don't be deceitful. You're not a scoundrel like the others. You are really fine, and you will stay. It wasn't for nothing I waited for you."

"You've gone mad!" he exclaimed sharply.

She looked up at him sternly, and even threatened him with her finger.

"That's not fine. Don't speak like that. When a truth comes to you, bow down humbly before it and do not say: 'You have gone mad.' That's what my author says, 'you've gone mad!' But you be honourable!"

"And what if I don't stay?" he asked with a wan smile, his lips distorted and pale.

"You will," she said with conviction. "Where can you go now? You have nowhere to go. You are honourable. I saw it the moment you kissed my hand. A fool, I thought, but honourable. You are not offended that I mistook you for a fool? It was your own fault. Well—why did you offer me your innocence? You thought: I will give her my innocence and she will renounce it. Oh, you fool! You fool! At first I was even offended. Why, I thought, he doesn't even consider me a human being! And then I saw that this, too, came from this fineness of yours. And this was your calculation: I pay her my innocence, and in return I shall be even purer than before and receive it back like a new shilling that hasn't been in circulation. I give it to the beggar and it will come back to me.... No, my dear, that game is not coming off!"

"N—not coming off?"

"N—no, dear," she drawled, "for I am not a fool. I've seen enough of these tradespeople. They pile up millions and then give a pound to a church and imagine they have righted themselves. No, dear, you must build me an entire church. You must give me the most precious thing you have, your innocence. Perhaps you are only giving up your innocence because it has become useless to you, because it has tarnished. Are you getting married?"

"No."

"Supposing you had a bride awaiting you tomorrow with flowers and embraces and love, then would you give away your innocence, or not?"

"I don't know," he said reflectively.

"This is what I mean. I should have said: Take my life, but leave me my honour. You would give away the cheaper of the two. But, no—you must give me the dearest thing of all, the thing without which you cannot live— that and nothing else!"

"But why should I give it away? Why?"

"Why? Only that it may not be shameful to you."

"But, Liuba!" he exclaimed in bewilderment. "Listen! You yourself are...."

"Fine, you were going to say? I've heard that too from my author, more than once. But, my dear, that is not the truth. I'm just an ordinary girl, and you will stay and then you will know it."

"I will not stay," he cried aloud, between his teeth.

"Don't shriek, my dear. Shrieks avail nothing against the truth—I know that for myself." And then in a whisper, looking straight in his eyes, she added: "For God, too, is fine!"

"Well, and then?"

"There's no more to be said. Think it out for yourself, and I'll stop talking. It's only five years since I went to church. That's the truth."

Truth? What truth? What was this unexplored terror, that he had never met before either in the face of death or in life itself? Truth?

Square-cheeked, hard-headed, conscious only of the conflict in his soul, he sat there resting his head on his hands and slowly turning his eyes as though from one extreme of life to the other. And life was collapsing—as a badly glued chest, rained upon in the autumn, falls into unrecognisable fragments of what had been so beautiful. He remembered the good fellows with whom he had lived his life and worked in a marvellous union of joy and sorrow—and they seemed strange to him and their life incomprehensible and their work senseless. It was as though someone with mighty fingers had taken hold of his soul and snapped it in two, as one snaps a stick across one's knee, and flung the fragments far apart. It was only a few hours since he left *there*—and all his life seemed to have been spent *here*, in front of this half-naked woman, listening to the distant music and the jingling of spurs; and that it would always be so. And he did not know which side to turn, up or down, but only that he was opposed, tormentingly opposed, to all that had that day become part of his very life and soul. Shameful to be fine....

He recalled the books which had taught him how to live, and he smiled bitterly. Books! There before him was one book, sitting with bare shoulders, closed eyes, an expression of beatitude on a pale distracted face, waiting patiently to be read to the end. Shameful to be fine....

And, all at once, with unbearable pain, grief-stricken, affrighted, he realized once and for all that that life was done with, that it had already become impossible for him to be fine!

He had only lived in that he was fine, it had been his only joy, and his only weapon in the battle of life and death.

All this was gone. Nothing was left. The Dark! Whether he stayed there or returned to his own people ... now, for him, his comrades were no more.

Why had he come to this accursed house! Better had he remained on the street, surrendered to the police, gone to prison where it was possible and even not disgraceful to be fine. And now it was too late even for prison.

"Are you crying?" the girl asked, perturbed.

"No," he answered curtly. "I never cry."

"And no need, dearie; we women can weep; you needn't. If you wept, too, who would there be to give an answer to God?"

She was his? This woman was his?

"Liuba," he cried in anguish, "what can I do? What can I do?"

"Stay with me. You can stay with me, for now you are mine."

"And They?"

The girl frowned.

"What sort of people are They?"

"Men! Men!" he exclaimed in a frenzy. "Men with whom I used to work. It was *not* for myself—no, *not* for self-satisfaction that I bore all this, that I was getting ready to carry out this assassination!"

"Don't talk to me about those people," she said sternly, though her lips trembled. "Don't mention them to me or I shall quarrel with you again. You hear me?"

"But what are you?" he asked amazed.

"I?—perhaps a cur! And all of us curs! But dearie, be careful! You've been able to take shelter behind us, and so be it. But do not try to hide from Truth; you will never elude her. If you must love mankind, then pity our sorry brotherhood."

She was sitting with her hands clasped behind her head, in an attitude of blissful repose, foolishly happy, almost beside herself. She moved her head from side to side, her eyes half closed in a daydream, spoke slowly, almost chanting her words.

"My own! My love! We will drink together! We will weep together. Oh, how delightful it will be to weep with you, dear one. I would so weep all my life. He has stayed with me. He has not gone away. When I saw him today, in the glass, it burst upon me at once: This is he!—my betrothed!— my darling! And I do not know who you are, brother or bridegroom of mine. But oh, so closely kin, so much desired...."

He, too, remembered that black dumb pair in the gilded mirror,—and the passing thought: as at a funeral. And all at once the whole thing became so intolerably painful, seemed so wild a nightmare, that he ground his teeth in his grief. His thoughts travelled farther back; he remembered his treasured revolver in his pocket, the two days of constant flight, the plain door that had no handle, and how he looked for a bell, and how a fat lackey who had not yet got his coat on straight had come out in a dirty printed linen shirt, and how he had entered with the proprietress into that white hall and seen those three strange girls.

And with it all a feeling of growing freedom came over him and at last he grasped that he was, as he had ever been, free—absolutely free—that he could go wherever he liked.

Sternly now he surveyed that strange room, severely, with the conviction of a man aroused for an instant from a debauch, seeing himself in foreign surroundings and condemning what he sees.

"What is all this? How idiotic! What a senseless nightmare!"

But—the music was still playing on. But—the woman was still sitting with her hands clasped behind her head, smiling, unable to speak, almost fainting under the load of a happiness beyond sense and experience. But— this was not a dream!

"What is all this? Is this—Truth?"

"Truth, my darling! You and I inseparable!"

This was Truth? Truth—those crumpled petticoats hanging on the wall in their bare disorder? Truth—that carpet on which thousands of drunken men had scuffled in spasms of hideous passion? Truth—this stale, moist fragrance, loathesomely cleaving to the face? Truth—that music and the jingling spurs? Truth—that woman with her pale and harassed face and smile of pitiful bliss?

Again he rested his heavy head on his hands, looking askance with the eyes of a wolf at bay; and his thoughts ran on without connection.

So she was Truth!... That meant that tomorrow and the day after he would not go, and everyone would know why he had not gone, that he had stayed with a girl, drinking; and they would call him traitor and coward and rascal. Some would intercede for him—would guess ... no, better not count on that, better see it all as it was! All over then? Was this the end? Into the dark—thus—into the dark? And what lay beyond? He did not know. In the dark? Probably some new horror. But then as yet he did not understand their ways. How strange that one had to learn to be common! And from whom? From her? No, she was no use. She didn't know anything. He would find out for himself. One had to become really common oneself in order to.... Yes, he would wreck something that was great! And then? And then, some day he would come back to her, or where they were drinking, or into a prison, and he would say: "Now I am not ashamed, now I am not guilty in any respect in your eyes. Now I am one like you, besmirched, fallen, unhappy!" Or he would go into the open street and say: "Look at me, what I am! I had everything—intellect, honour, dignity—stranger still, immortality. And all this I flung at the feet of a whore. I renounced it all because she was common!" What would they say? They would gape, and be astounded, and say, "What a fool!" Yes—yes, a fool! Was he guilty because he was fine? Let her—let everyone—try to be fine! "Sell all thou hast and give to the poor." But that was just what he had done, all that he had. But this was Christ—in whom he did not believe.... Or perhaps.... "He who loses his soul"—not his life, but his soul.... That was what he was contemplating. Perhaps ... did Christ himself sin with the sinners, commit adultery, get drunk? No, he only forgave those who did, and even loved them. Well, so did he love and forgive and pity her. Then, why sacrifice himself? For she was not of the faith. Nor he. Nor was this Christ; but something else, something more dreadful.

"Oh, this is dreadful, Liuba!"

"Dreadful, darling? Yes, it is dreadful to see Truth."

Truth—again she named it! But what made it dreadful? Why should he dread what he so desired? No—no—there was nothing to fear. There, in the open, in front of all those gaping mouths, would he not be the highest of them all? Though naked and dirty and ragged—and his face would be horrible then—he who had lost abandoned himself, would he not be the terrible proclaimer of justice eternal, to which God himself must submit—otherwise he were not God?

"There is nothing dreadful about it, Liuba."

"Yes, darling, there is. You are not afraid, and that is well. But do not provoke it. There is no need to do that."

"So that is it—that is my end! It is not what I expected—not what I expected for the end of my young and beautiful life. My God, but this is senseless! I must have gone mad! Still it is not too late ... not too late ... I can still escape."

"My darling," the woman was murmuring, her hands still clasped behind her head.

He glanced at her and frowned. Her eyes were blissfully closed; a happy, unthinking smile upon her lips expressed an unquenchable thirst, an insatiable hunger, as though she had just tasted something and was preparing for more.

He looked down on her and frowned—on her thin soft arms, on the dark hollows of her armpits; and he got up without any haste. With a last effort to save something precious—life or reason, or the good old Truth—without any flurry, but solemnly, he began dressing himself. He could not find his collar.

"Tell me, have you seen my collar?"

"Where are you going?" The woman looked round. Her hands fell away from her head, and the whole of her strained forward towards him.

"I am going away."

"You are going away?" she repeated, dragging the words. "You are going? Where?"

He smiled derisively.

"As if I had nowhere to go! I am going to my comrades."

"To the fine folk? Have you cheated me?"

"Yes. To the fine folk." Again the same smile. He had finished dressing, he was feeling his pockets.

"Give me my pocket-book."

She handed it to him.

"And my watch."

She gave it to him. They had been lying together on the little table.

"Goodbye."

"Are you frightened?"

The question was quiet and simple. He looked up. There stood a woman, tall and shapely, with thin, almost child-like arms, a pale smile, and blanched lips, asking: "Are you frightened?"

How strangely she could change! Sometimes forceful and even terrible, she was now pathetic and more like a girl than a woman. But all this was of no account. He stepped toward the door.

"But I thought you were going to stay...."

"What?"

"The key's in your pocket—for my sake."

The lock was already creaking.

"Very well, then! Go ... go to your comrades and...."

It was then, at the last moment, when he had nothing to do but to open the door and go out and seek his comrades and end a noble life with a heroic death—it was then he committed the wild, incomprehensible act that ruined his life. It may have been a frenzy that sometimes unaccountably seizes hold of the strongest and calmest minds; or it may have been actually that, through the drunken scraping of a fiddle somewhere in that bawdy house, through the sorcery of the downcast eyes of a prostitute, he discovered a last new terrible truth of life, a truth of his own, which none other could see and understand. Whichever it were—insanity or revelation, lies or truth, this new understanding of his—he accepted it manfully and unconditionally, with that inflexible spirit which had drawn his previous life along one straight, fiery line, directing its flight like the feathers on an arrow.

He passed his hand slowly, very slowly, over his hard, bristly skull, and, without even shutting the door, simply returned and sat in his former place on the bed. His broad cheekbones, his paleness, made him look more than ever a foreigner.

"What's the matter? Have you forgotten something?"

The girl was astonished. She no longer expected anything.

"No."

"What is it? Why don't you go?"

Quietly, with the expression of a stone on which life has engraved one last commandment, grim and new, he answered:

"I do not wish to be fine."

She still waited, not daring to believe, suddenly shrinking from what she had so much sought and yearned for. She knelt down. He smiled gently, and in the same new and impressive manner stood over her and placed his hand on her head and repeated:

"I do not want to be fine."

The woman busied herself swiftly in her joy. She undressed him like a child, unlaced his boots, fumbling at the knots, stroked his head, his knees, and never so much as smiled—so full was her heart. Then she looked up into his face and was afraid.

"How pale you are! Drink something now—at once! Are you feeling ill, Peter?"

"My name is Alexis."

"Never mind that. Here, let me give you some in a glass. Well, take care then; don't choke yourself! If you're not used to it, it's not so easy as out of a glass."

She opened her mouth, seeing him drink with slow, sceptical gulps. He coughed.

"Never mind! You'll be a good drinker, I can see that! Oh, how happy I am!"

With an animal cry she leapt on him, and began smothering him with short, vigorous kisses, to which he had no time to respond. It was funny— she was a stranger, yet kissed so hard! He held her firmly for a moment, held her immovable, and was silent awhile, himself motionless—held her as though he too felt the strength of quiescence, the strength of a woman, as his own strength. And the woman, joyously, obediently, became limp in his arms.

"So be it!" he said, with an imperceptible sigh.

The woman bestirred herself anew, burning in the savagery of her joy as in a fire. Her movements filled the room, as if she were not one but a score of half-witted women who spoke, stirred, went to and fro, kissed him. She plied him with cognac, and drank more herself. Then a sudden recollection seized her; she clasped her hands.

"But the revolver—we forgot that! Give it to me—quick, quick! I must take it to the office."

"Why?"

"Oh, I'm scared of the thing! Would it go off at once?"

He smiled, and repeated:

"Would it go off at once? Yes, it would. At once!"

He took out his revolver, and, deliberately weighing in his hand that silent and obedient weapon, gave it to the girl. He also handed her the cartridge clips.

"Take them!"

When he was left alone and without the revolver he had carried so many years, the half open door letting in the sound of strange voices and the clink of spurs, he felt the whole weight of the great burden he had taken on his shoulders. He walked silently across the room in the direction where They were to be found, and said one word:

"Well?"

A chill came over him as he crossed his arms, facing Them; and that one little word held many meanings—a last farewell—some obscure challenge, some irrevocable evil resolution to fight everyone, even his own comrades—a little, a very little, sense of reproach.

He was still standing there when Liuba ran in, excitedly calling to him from the door.

"Dearie, dearie, now don't be angry. I've asked my friends here, some of them. You don't mind? You see, I want so much to show them my sweetheart, my darling; you don't mind? They're dears! Nobody has taken them this evening and they're all alone. The officers have gone to bed now. One of them noticed your revolver and liked it. A very fine one, he said. You don't mind? You don't mind, dear?" And the girl smothered him with short, sharp kisses.

The women were already coming in, chattering and simpering—five or six of the ugliest or oldest of the establishment—painted, with drooping eyes, their hair combed up over their brows. Some of them affected attitudes of shame, and giggled; others quietly eyed the cognac, and looking at him earnestly shook hands. Apparently they had already been to bed; they were all in scanty wrappers; one very fat woman, indolent and indifferent, had come in nothing but a petticoat, her bare arms and corpulent bosom incredibly fat. This fat woman, and another one with an evil bird-like aged face, on which the white paint lay like dirty stucco on a wall, were quite drunk; the others were merry. All this mob of women, half naked, giggling, surrounded him; and an intolerable stench of bodies and stale beer rose and mingled with the clammy, soapy air of the room. A sweating lackey hurried in with cognac, dressed in a tight frocks coat much too small for him, and the girls greeted him with a chorus of:

"Màrkusha! Oh, Màrkusha! Dear Màrkusha!"

Apparently it was a custom of the house to greet him with such exclamations, for even the fat drunken woman murmured lazily, "Màrkusha!"

They drank and clinked glasses, all talking at once about affairs of their own. The evil-looking woman with the bird-like face was irritably and noisily telling of a guest who took her for a time ... and then something had happened. There was much interchange of gutterswords and phrases, pronounced not with the indifference of men, but with a peculiar asperity, even acidity; and every object was called by its proper name.

At first they paid little heed to him, and he maintained an obstinate silence, merely looking on. Liuba, full of her happiness, sat quietly beside him on the bed, one arm about his neck, herself drinking little, but constantly plying him, and from time to time whispering in his ear, "Darling!"

He drank heavily, but it did not make him tipsy; what was happening in him was something different, something which strong alcohol often secretly effects. Whilst he drank and sat there silent, the work was going on in him, vast, destructive, swift, and numbing. It was as though all he had known in his past life, all he had loved and meditated—talks with companions, books, perilous and alluring tasks—was noiselessly being burned, annihilated without a trace, and he himself not injured in the process, but rather made stronger and harder. With every glass he drank he seemed to return to some earlier self of his, to some primitive rebel ancestor, for whom rebellion was religion and religion rebellion. Like a colour being washed away in boiling water, his foreign bookish wisdom was fading and was being replaced by something of his very own, wild and dark as the black earth—from whose bleak stretches, from the infinitudes of slumbrous forest and boundless plain, blew the wind that was the life-breath of this ultimate blind wisdom of his; and in this wind could be heard the tumultuous jangling of bells, and through it could be seen the blood-red dawn of great fires, and the clank of iron fetters, and the rapture of prayer, and the Satanic laughter of myriad giant throats; and above his uncovered head the murky dome of the sky.

Thus he sat. Broad cheeked, pallid, already quite at home with these miserable creatures racketing around him. And, in his soul, laid waste by the conflagration of a desolated world, there glowed and gleamed, like a white fire of incandescent steel, one thing alone—his flaming will; blind now and purposeless, it was still greedily reaching out afar, while his body, undisturbed, was secretly being steeled in the feeling of limitless power and ability to create all things or to shatter all things at will.

Suddenly he hammered on the table with his fist.

"Drink, Liubka! Drink!"

And when, radiant and smiling, she had poured herself out a glass, he lifted his, and cried aloud.

"Here's to our Brotherhood!"

"You mean Them?" whispered Liuba.

"No, these. To our Brotherhood! To the blackguards, brutes and cowards, to those who are crushed by life, to those perishing from syphilis, to...."

The other girls laughed, the fat one indolently objecting:

"Oh, come, that's going a bit too far, my dear!"

"Hush!" said Liuba, turning very pale, "He is my betrothed."

"To those who are blind from birth! Ye who can see, pluck out your eyes! For it is shameful"—and he banged on the table—"it is shameful for those who have sight to look upon those who are blind from birth! If with our light we cannot illumine all the darkness, then let us put out the signal fires, let us all crawl in the dark! If there be not paradise for all, then I will have none for myself! And this, girls, this is no part of paradise, but simply and plainly a piggery! A toast, girls! That all the signal fires be extinguished. Drink! To the Dark!"

He staggered a little as he drank off his glass. He spoke rather thickly, but firmly, precisely, with pauses, enunciating every syllable. Nobody understood his wild speech, but they found him pleasing in himself, his pale figure and his peculiar quality of wickedness. Then Liuba suddenly took up the word, stretching out her hands.

"He is my betrothed. He will stay with me. He was virtuous and had comrades, and now he will stay with me!"

"Come and take Màrkusha's place," the fat woman drawled.

"Shut up, Manka, or I'll smash your face! He will stay with me. He was virtuous...."

"We were all virtuous once," the evil old woman grumbled. And the others joined in: "I was straight four years ago ... I'm an honourable woman still ... I swear to God...."

Liuba was nearly weeping.

"Silence, you sluts! You had your honour taken from you; but he gives it me himself. He takes it and gives it for my honour. But I don't want honour! You're a lot of ... and he's still an innocent boy!"

She broke into sobs. There was a general outburst of laughter. They guffawed as only the drunken can, without any restraint; the little room, saturated with sounds, and unable to absorb any more, threw it all back in a deafening roar. They laughed until the tears fell; they rolled together and groaned with it. The fat woman clucked in a little thin voice and tumbled exhausted from her chair.

And, last of all, he laughed out loud at the sight of them.

It was as though the Satanic world itself had foregathered there to laugh to its grave that little sprig of virtue, the dead innocence itself joining in the laughter.

The only one who did not laugh was Liuba. Trembling with agitation, she wrung her hands and shouted at them, and finally flung herself with her fists on the fat woman, who even with her beam-like arms could hardly ward off her blows.

"So be it!" he shouted in his laughter. But the others could hear nothing.

At last the noise died down a little.

"So be it!" he cried, a second time. "But, peace! Silence!—I have something to show you!"

"Leave them alone," said Liuba, wiping her tears away with her fist. "We must get rid of them."

Still shaking with laughter he turned round to face her.

"Are you frightened?" he asked. "Was it honour you wanted after all? You fool! It's the only thing you ever have wanted! Leave me alone!"

Without taking any more notice of her, he addressed himself to the others, rising and holding his closed hands above his head.

"Listen! I'll show you something! Look here, at my hands!"

Merry and curious, they looked at his hands, and waited obediently, like children, with gaping mouths.

"Here! Here! See?" He shook his hands. "I hold my life in my hands! Do you see?"

"Yes! Yes! Go on!"

"My life was noble, it was! It was pure and beautiful. Yes, it was! It was like those pretty porcelain vases. And now, look! I fling it away...." He let fall his hands, almost with a groan, and all their eyes looked downwards as though there really lay something down there, something delicate and brittle, that had been shattered into fragments—a beautiful human life.

"Trample on it, now, girls! Trample it to pieces until not a bit of it is left!"

Like children enjoying a new game, with a whoop and a laugh, they leapt up and began trampling on the spot where lay the fragments of that invisible dainty porcelain, a beautiful human life. Gradually a new frenzy overcame them. The laughter and shrieks died away, and nothing but their heavy breathing was audible above the continuous stamping and clatter of feet—rabid, unrelenting, implacable.

Liuba, like an affronted queen, watched it a moment over his shoulder with savage eyes; then suddenly, as though she had only just understood and been driven mad, with a wild groan of elation she burst into the midst of the jostling women and joined the trampling in a faster measure. But for the earnestness of the drunken faces, the ferocity of the bleary eyes, the wickedness of the depraved and twisted mouths, it might all have been taken for some new kind of dance without music, without rhythm.

With his fingers gripping into his hard bristly skull, the man looked on, calm and grim.

Two voices were speaking in the dark—Liuba's, intimate, tentative, sensitive, with delicate intonations of private apprehension such as a woman's voice always gains in the dark, and his hard, quiet, distant. He spoke his words too precisely, too harshly—the only sign of intoxication not quite passed away.

"Are your eyes open?" she asked.

"Yes."

"Are you thinking about something?"

"Yes."

Silence—and the dark. Then again the thoughtful, vigilant voice of the woman.

"Tell me something more about your comrades, will you?"

"What for?... They—they were."

He said WERE as the living speak of the dead, or as the dead might speak of the living, and through the even course of his calm and almost indifferent narration it resounded like a funeral knell, as though he were an old man telling his children the heroic tale of a long departed past. And, in the darkness, before the girl's enchanted eyes, there rose the image of a little group of young men, pitifully young, bereft of father and mother, and hopelessly hostile both to the world they were fighting and to the world they were fighting for. Having travelled by dream to the distant future, to the land of brotherly men as yet unborn, they lived their short lives like pale blood-stained shadows or spectres, the scarecrows of humanity. And their lives were stupidly short—the gallows awaited every one of them, or penal servitude, or insanity—nothing else to look forward to but prison, the scaffold, or the madhouse. And there were women among them....

Liuba started and raised herself on her elbows.

"Women? What do you mean, darling?"

"Young, gentle girls, still in their teens. They follow in the steps of the men, manfully, daringly, die with them...."

"Die! Oh my God!" she cried, clutching his shoulder.

"What? Are you touched by this?"

"Never mind, darling. I sometimes.... Go on with your story! Go on!"

And he went on with his story, and there happened a wonderful thing. Ice was turned into fire. Through the funeral notes of hi requiem speech, suddenly rang for the girl, her eyes wide open now and burning, the gospel of a new, joyous, and mighty life. Tears rose in her eyes and dried there as in a furnace; she was excited to the pitch of rebellion, eager for every word. Like a hammer upon glowing iron, his words were forging in her a new responsive soul Steadily, regularly, it fell—beating the soul ever to a finer temper—and suddenly, in the suffocating stench of that room, there spoke aloud a new and unknown voice, the voice of a human being.

"Darling, am I not also a woman?"

"What do you mean?"

"I also might go with Them?"

He did not reply, and in his silence he seemed to her so remarkable and so great (he had been Their comrade, had lived with Them) that it felt uncomfortable to be lying beside him, embracing him. She moved away a little and left only a hand touching him, so that the contact might be less; and forgetting her hatred of the Fine, her tears and curses, and the long years of inviolable solitude in the depths—overcome by the beauty and self-denial of Their lives—her face flushed with excitement, and she was ready to weep at the terrible thought that They might not accept her.

"Dear, but will they take me? My God, if they won't! What do you think? Tell me they'll take me—they won't be squeamish! They won't say: You are impossible, you are vile, you have sold yourself! Answer me!"

Silence—and then a reply that rejoiced.

"Yes, they will! Why not, indeed?"

"Oh, my darling. But...."

"Fine people, they are!" The man's voice had the finality of a big fat full stop, but the girl triumphantly repeated, with a touching confidence:

"Yes! They are fine!"

And so radiant was her smile that it seemed as if the very darkness smiled in sympathy and some little stars strayed in as well, little blue points of light. For a new truth had reached her—one that brought not fear, but joy.

Then the shy suppliant voice.

"Let us go to them, dear? You'll take me with you? You won't be ashamed of having such a companion? For they'll accept me, won't they? Just as you did when you came here? Surely you were driven here for some purpose! But—to stay here—you would simply drop into the cesspool. As for me, I—I—I will try. Why don't you say anything?"

Grim silence again, in which could be heard the beating of two hearts— one rapid, hurried, excited; the other hard and slow, strongely slow.

"Would you be shamed to go back with such as me?"

A stern prolonged silence, and then a reply, solid and inflexible as unpolished rock:

"I am not going back. I don't want to be fine."

Silence. Then presently:

"They are gentlemen," he said, and his voice sounded solitary and strained.

"Who?" she asked, dully.

"They—Those who were."

A long silence—this time as though a bird had thrown itself down and was falling, whirling through the air on its pliant wings, but unable to reach the earth, unable to strike the ground and lie at rest.

In the dark he knew that Liuba, silently, carefully, making the least stir possible, passed over him; was busying herself with something.

"What are you doing?"

"I don't like lying there like that. I want to get dressed."

Then she must have put something on and sat down; for the chair creaked ever so little; and it became so still—as silent as though the room were empty. The stillness lasted a long time; and then the calm, serious voice spoke:

"I think, Liuba, there is still one cognac left on the table. Take a drink and come and lie down again."

Day was already dawning, and in the house all was as quiet as in any other house, when the police appeared. After long arguments and hesitations Mark had been dispatched to the police station with the revolver and cartridges and a circumstantial account of the strange visitor. The police at once guessed who he was. For three days they had had him on their nerves. They had been seeing him here, there, and everywhere; but finally, all trace of him had been lost. Somebody had suggested searching the brothels of the district; but just then somebody else got another false clue, so the public resorts were forgotten.

The telephone tinkled excitedly. Half an hour later, in the chill of the October morning, heavy boots were scrunching the hoar-frost and along the empty streets moved in silence a company of policemen and detectives. In front of them, feeling in every inch of his body what a mistake it was to take the risks of such exposure, marched the district superintendent, an elderly man, very tall, in a thick official overcoat, the shape of a sack. He was yawning, burying his flabby red nose in his grey whiskers; and he was thinking that he ought to wait for the military; that it was nonsense to go for such a man without soldiers, with nothing but stupid drowsy policemen who didn't know how to shoot. More than once he reached the point of calling himself the slave of duty, yawning every time long and heavily.

The superintendent was a drunkard, a regular debauchee of the resorts of his district; and they paid him heavily for the right to exist. He had no desire to die. When they called him from his bed, he had nursed his revolver for a long time from one greasy palm to the other, and although there was little time to spare he had ordered them to clean his jacket, as though for a review. That very night at the police station, he remembered, conversation had turned on this same man who had been dodging them all, and the superintendent, with the cynicism of an old sot, had called the man a hero and himself an old police trollop. When his assistants laughed, he had assured them that such heroes must exist, if only to be hanged. "You hang him—and it pleases you both: him because he is going straight to the Kingdom of Heaven, and you as a demonstration that brave men still exist. Don't snigger—it's true."

On that chill October morning, marching along the cold streets, he appreciated clearly that the talk of yesterday was lies; that the man was nothing but a rascal. He was ashamed of his own boyish extravagance.

"A hero, indeed!" the superintendent prayerfully recanted. "Lord, if he so much as stirs a finger, the blackguard, I'll kill him like a dog. By God, I will!"

And that set him thinking why he, the superintendent, an old man full of gout, so much desired to live. Because there was hoar frost on the streets? He turned round and shouted savagely: "Quick march, there! Don't go like sheep!"

The wind blew into his overcoat. His jacket was too wide and his whole body quivered in it like the yolk of an egg in a stirring basin. He felt as if he was suddenly shrinking. The palms of his hands, despite the cold, were still sweaty.

They surrounded the house as though they had come to take not one sleeper but a host in ambush. Then some of them crept along the dark corridor on tiptoe to the fearsome door.

A desperate knock—a shout—threats to shoot through the door. And when, almost knocking Liuba, half naked, off her feet, they burst into the little room in close formation and filled it with their boots and cloaks and rifles—then they saw him—sitting on the bed in his shirt, with his bare hairy legs hanging down—sitting there silent. No bomb—nothing terrible— nothing but the ordinary room of a prostitute, filthy and repulsive in the early morning light, with its stretch of tattered carpet and scattered clothes, the table smeared and stained with liquor—and sitting on the bed a man, clean shaven and with drowsy eyes, high cheekbones, a swollen face, hairy legs—silent.

"Hands up!" shouted the superintendent, holding his revolver tighter in his damp hand.

But the man neither raised his arms nor made any answer.

"Search him!" the superintendent ordered.

"There's nothing to search! I took his revolver away. Oh, my God!" Liuba cried, her teeth chattering with fear. She had nothing on but a crumpled chemise; among the others, all wrapped in their cloaks, the two, man and woman, both half naked, roused feelings of shame, disgust, and contempt.

They searched his clothing, ransacked the carpet, peered into the corners, into the cupboard, and found nothing.

"I took his revolver from him," Liuba thoughtlessly insisted.

"Silence Liubka!" the superintendent shouted. He knew the girl well, had spent two or three nights with her. He believed her; but his relief was so unexpected that out of sheer pleasure he wanted to shout and command and show his authority.

"Your name?"

"I shall not say. I shall not answer any questions at all."

"All right, sir, all right," the superintendent replied ironically, but somewhat abashed. Then he looked again at the naked hairy feet and at the girl shuddering in the corner, and suddenly became suspicious.

"Is this the right man?" he said, taking a detective aside. "Something seems...."

The detective went and stared closely in the man's face, then nodded his head decisively.

"Yes. It's he. He's only shaved his beard. You can recognise him by his cheekbones."

"A brigand's cheekbones, sure enough."

"And look at the eyes, too. I could pick him out of a thousand by his eyes."

"His eyes? Let me see the photograph."

He took a long look at the unfinished proof photograph of a man, very handsome, wonderfully pure and young, with a long bushy Russian beard. The expression on the face was the same. Not grim, but very calm and bright. The cheekbones were not markedly prominent.

"You see! His cheekbones don't stand out like...."

"They are concealed by the beard, but if you feel under it with the eye...."

"It may be, but.... Is he a hard drinker?"

The detective, tall and thin, with a yellow face and sparse beard, himself a hard drinker, smiled patronizingly.

"There's no drinking among them."

"I know there isn't but still...." The superintendent approached the man. "Listen! Were you an accomplice in the murder of N——?" It was a very important and well known name.

But the man remained silent and only smiled and fidgeted with one hairy leg; the toes were bent and distorted by boots.

"You are being examined!"

"You may as well leave him alone. He won't reply. We'd better wait for the captain and prosecutor. They'll make him talk."

The superintendent smiled, but in his heart for some reason he felt the shrinking again.

They had been tearing up the carpet; they had upset something, and there was a very unpleasant smell in the ill-ventilated room.

"What filth!" thought the superintendent, though in the matter of cleanliness he was by no means nice. And he looked with disgust at that naked swinging foot. "So he is still fidgeting with his foot," he thought.

He turned round; a young policeman, with pure white eye-lashes and eyebrows, was sneering at Liuba, holding his rifle with both hands as a village night watchman holds his staff.

"Well, Liubka," the superintendent cried, approaching her. "Why didn't you report at once who you had with you, you bitch?"

"Oh, I was...."

The superintendent smacked her face twice, quite neatly, first on one cheek then on the other.

"Take that then! I'll show you!"

The man's brows went up and the foot ceased swinging.

"So you don't like that, young fellow?" The contempt of the superintendent was growing apace. "What are you going to do about it? You kissed this face, didn't you, and we'll do what we damn well...."

He laughed, and the policeman smiled in some agitation. And what was more surprising, even the downtrodden Liuba laughed. She looked at the old superintendent in a friendly way, as though she enjoyed his jokes and jollity.

From the moment of the arrival of the police she had never looked at the man, betraying him naturally and openly; and this he saw, and was silent and smiled half scoffingly, a strange smile—as a gray stone in the forest, sunk into the ground and mossgrown, might smile.

Half dressed women were crowding about the door, amongst them some of those who had visited them. But they looked at him indifferently, with a dull curiosity, as though this was the first time they had seen him.

Apparently they remembered nothing of the night. They were soon hustled away.

It was now daylight, and the room was more bleak and repulsive than ever. Two officers who evidently had not had their full sleep came in, their faces ruffled, but properly dressed and clean.

"It's no good, gentlemen, really," the superintendent said with a spiteful glance at the man. The officers approached, looked him up and down from his crown to his naked feet with those bent toes, surveyed Liuba, and casually exchanged observations.

"Yes—he's good looking," said the young one, the one who had invited them all to the cotillion. He had splendid white teeth and silky whiskers and soft eyes with girlish lashes. He looked at the arrested man with disdainful compassion, and wrinkled his eyes as if he were going to cry. There was a corn on the left little toe ... somehow it was horrible and disgusting to see that little yellow mound. And the legs were dirty. "This is a fine pass for you to come to, sir," he said, shaking his head and painfully contracting his brows.

"So that's how it is, Mr. Anarchist? You're no better than us sinners with the girls? The flesh was weak, eh?" jeered the other, the elder.

"Why did you give up your revolver? You might at least have had a shot for it. I understand that you found yourself here, as anyone might find himself; but why did you give up your revolver? A poor example to set your comrades!" said the little officer, hotly; and then explained to the elder: "He had a Browning with three cartridge clips. Just think of it! Stupid!"

But the man, smiling contemptuously from the height of his new, unmeasured, and terrible truth, looked on the little excited officer and indifferently kept on swinging his leg. The fact of his being nearly naked, of having dirty hairy legs with bent and crooked toes, gave him no sense of shame. Had they taken him just as he was and planted him in the most populous square of the city, in front of all the men and women and children, he would have gone on dangling that hairy leg with the same equanimity, smiling the same disdainful smile.

"Do they know what comradeship is?" said the superintendent. He was savagely looking askance at that swaying leg, and indolently trying to dissuade the officers. "It's no good talking to him, gentlemen, I swear! No good! You know the kind of thing—instructions!"

Other officers entered quite freely, surveyed the scene and chatted together. One of them, evidently an old acquaintance of the superintendent, shook hands with him. Liuba was already coquetting with the officers.

"Just imagine! A Browning with three clips and, like a fool, he gave it up!" the little officer was relating. "I can't understand that!"

"You, Misha, will never understand this."

"For, after all, they are no cowards!"

"You, Misha, are an idealist, and the milk has not yet dried on your lips."

"Samson and Delilah," one short snuffling officer said ironically; he had a little drooping nose and thin whiskers combed back and upwards.

"Oh Delilah! What a smiler!"

They laughed.

The superintendent, smiling pleasantly and rubbing his flabby red nose downwards, suddenly approached the man and stood as if to screen him from the officers with his own carcase encased in the loose hanging coat; and he murmured under his breath, rolling his eyes wildly:

"Shameful, sir! You might at least have put your drawers on, sir! Shameful! And a hero, too? Involved with a prostitute ... with this carrion-flesh? What will your comrades say of you,—eh, you cur?"

Liuba, stretching her naked neck, heard him. They were together now, side by side, these three plain truths of life, the corrupt old drunkard who yearned for heroes, the dissolute woman into whose soul some scattered seeds of purpose and self-denial had fallen—and the man. After the superintendent's words, he paled slightly, and seemed to wish to say something—but changed his mind and smiled, and went on swinging that hairy leg.

The officers wandered off; the police accommodated themselves to the situation, to the presence of the half naked couple, and stood about sleepily, with that absence of visible thought which renders the faces of all guards alike.

The superintendent put his hands on the table and pondered deeply and sadly—that he would not get a nap today, that he would have to go to the station and set matters on foot. But something else made him even more melancholy and weary.

"May I dress myself?" asked Liuba.

"No!"

"I'm cold."

"Never mind—sit as you are!"

The superintendent didn't even look at her. So she turned away, and, stretching out her thin neck, whispered something to the man, softly, with her lips only. He raised his brows in enquiry, and she repeated:

"Darling! My Darling!"

He nodded and smiled affectionately. Then seeing him smile to to her so gently, though plainly forgetting nothing—seeing him, who was so handsome and proud, now naked and despised by all, with his dirty bare legs, she was suddenly flushed with a feeling of unbearable love and demoniac blind wrath. She gasped, and flung herself on her knees on that damp floor, and embraced those cold hairy feet.

"Dress yourself, darling!" she murmured in an ecstasy. "Dress yourself!"

"Liubka, stop this!" The superintendent dragged her away. "He's not worth it!"

The girl sprang to her feet.

"Silence, you old profligate! He's better than the whole lot of you put together!"

"He's a swine!"

"You're a swine!"

"What?" The superintendent promptly lost his temper. "Tackle her, my man! Hold her down. Leave your rifle alone, you block-head!"

"Oh, darling, why did you give up your revolver?" the girl moaned, struggling with the policeman. "Why didn't you bring a bomb? We might have ... might have ... them all to...."

"Gag her!"

The panting woman struggled desperately, trying to bite the rough fingers that were holding her. The policeman with the white eye-lashes, disconcerted, not knowing how to fight a woman, was seizing her by her hair, by her breasts, trying to fling her on the ground and sniffing in his desperation.

From the corridor new voices were heard, loud, unconcerned, and the jangle of a police officer's spurs. A sweet, sincere, barytone voice was leading, as though a star was making his entrance and now at last the real and serious opera was about to commence.

The superintendent pulled his coat straight.